WHO POOED IN MY LOO?

Emma Adams   Mike Byrne

SCHOLASTIC

In the bathroom this morning, I looked in the loo,
and guess what I saw – yes that's right, it's **a poo!**
I couldn't believe it, I called for my mum,

"There's a gift in our toilet . . . made by a **bum!**"

Quick as a flash, I knew just what to do – someone had **pooped** here and **I'd find out WHO!**

Maybe a **dinosaur** stamped in, **STOMP** *STOMP,*
and sat on the toilet with one giant

WHOMP!

Then ate all the loo paper, even a towel,
before rumbling out on a neighbourhood prowl.

Or . . .

HET/CH

We hope you enjoy this book.
Please return or renew it by the due date.
You can renew it at **www.norfolk.gov.uk/libraries**
or by using our free library app. Otherwise you can
phone **0344 800 8020** - please have your library
card and pin ready.
You can sign up for email reminders too.

NORFOLK COUNTY COUNCIL
LIBRARY AND INFORMATION SERVICE

This book is dedicated to some of the
most brilliant children I know, including
Freddy Thomas Bonner and Ronnie Stewart Bonner,
Florence Lily Hodgkins,
James Edward Kilgarriff and Adeline Jane Kilgarriff,
Anya Elizabeth Ramshaw,
and Edina Jane Whittaker,

EA

To Oscar & Harry, who bear more than
a passing resemblance to the two brothers
and whose poos I usually find in my loo!

MB

First published in 2020 by Scholastic Children's Books
Euston House, 24 Eversholt Street
London NW1 1DB
a division of Scholastic Ltd
www.scholastic.co.uk

London – New York – Toronto – Sydney – Auckland
Mexico City – New Delhi – Hong Kong

PB ISBN 978 0702 30383 8

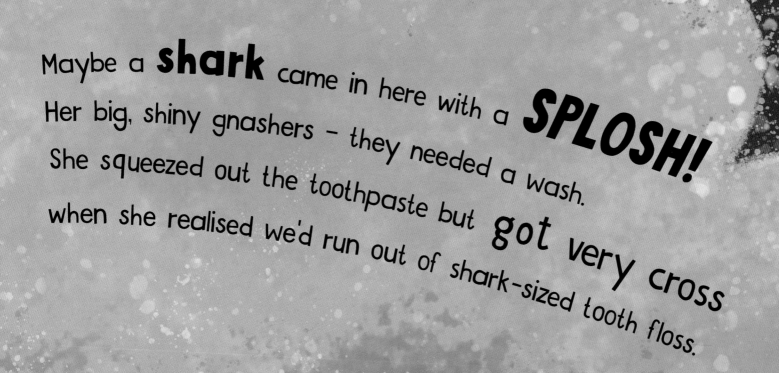

Maybe a **shark** came in here with a **SPLOSH!**
Her big, shiny gnashers – they needed a wash.
She squeezed out the toothpaste but **got very cross**
when she realised we'd run out of shark-sized tooth floss.

Maybe a **dragon** flew in with a **SWOOP**

to sit on our toilet for his **morning poop.**

He stretched out his wings and gave my dad a scare when he flew out the door breathing fire **everywhere.** Or . . . .

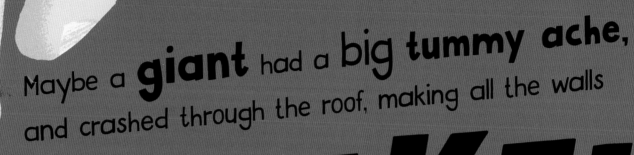

Maybe a **giant** had a big **tummy ache**,
and crashed through the roof, making all the walls

SHAKE!

But that can't be right, I realise with a snigger.
A giant's poo? Well, that would be

much, much bigger!

Did an **elephant** sit in the bath with a **CLUNK** then spurt lots of **water** from his **giant trunk**? Did he use all the soap, and the bubble bath too, before realising he needed the loo?

What if a **lion** padded in with a . . .

ROAR

feeling upset cos his **bottom** was sore.

I bet he growled **loudly** and shook out his mane.

He probably ate too much breakfast again.

Or . . .

Maybe the poo was left here by an **elf**
who sat on our **toilet** instead of a **shelf**,
singing "Frosty the Snowman" and then "Jingle Bells".
Hey, Elf, those are **not** very Christmassy smells!

Oh look!

There's a **rainbow** outside, shining bright.

Maybe a **unicorn** came in the night.

Shining with magic, like unicorns do. Although . . .

this does **not** look like **magical poo.**

No, it **can't** be a **unicorn**, **shark** or **big cat**,
a **dragon** or **elephant** – nothing like that.

Not a **dino** or **giant** or **elf** – but then who?

Who left this poo in our family loo?

But, now that I think of it, there **is** one other . . .
He lives in this house, yes, you've got it . . . .

... My brother!

You see, he's still learning, and he's only three, he's not quite as big or as grown-up as me.

"I'm sorry I left it," he says with a blush,
"It's alright," I say, "but remember to flush!
And wash both your hands very carefully too
whenever you go for a wee or a poo."